The Bedtime Beast

written by Rose Impey
illustrated by Sue Porter

HEINEMANN : LONDON

Most of the time my brother Tom is no trouble at all. He plays and reads and watches television.

We all kiss him goodnight.
Then Dad tucks him in . . .

. . . but Tom gets out.

I read him *five* stories . . .

. . . but he still says, 'More!'

He calls down, 'Mum,
put the light on.'

'Dad, can I have a drink?'

'I want to wee.'

Mum and Dad say,

'Tom, go to sleep.'

Mum and Dad are too tired
to move. They let him play.
He loves it.

I bet he would stay awake
all night if they'd let him.